KU-574-665

LITTLE MISS
BIRTHDAY

Roger Hargreaves

Original concept by
Roger Hargreaves

Written and illustrated by
Adam Hargreaves

EGMONT

Little Miss Birthday enjoys every day because every day is someone's birthday and Little Miss Birthday loves birthday presents! She loves choosing presents, she loves wrapping presents, and she loves giving presents.

And she is very good at choosing presents. Little Miss Birthday prides herself on always picking the perfect present.

However fussy the person might be.

Last year, she gave Mr Fussy a tiny iron for ironing his shoe laces. It was exactly what he wanted. Nobody is sure if they have ever seen Mr Fussy look quite so happy.

She gave Little Miss Star a radio which gives her a round of applause every time she turns it on.

And she gave Mr Bump a bed with no legs. No more going bump in the night for Mr Bump when he falls out of bed!

Little Miss Birthday has a birthday book to help her keep track of everyone's birthday.

A very big birthday book.

Last week, Little Miss Birthday was leafing through her book to see whose birthdays were coming up.

"Mr Lazy," she read out loud. "Easy peasy. I will give Mr Lazy an alarm clock with a silent alarm. Now, who is next? Mr Wrong."

A puzzled expression settled across Little Miss Birthday's face. She could not think of anything to give to Mr Wrong.

"Just think harder," she told herself.

But the harder she thought, the more puzzled she became. Little Miss Birthday did not have a clue what to give Mr Wrong for his birthday.

Everything she could think of would be wrong!

The next day, she had plenty of time to ponder this problem because it was Little Miss Late's birthday and Little Miss Late, it won't surprise you to hear, was late for her own birthday.

When she finally turned up, she loved her present.

A bus stop.

No more running to the bus stop to catch the bus, she now always has one with her!

That night, Little Miss Birthday hardly slept a wink. Mr Wrong's birthday was drawing closer and she still had no idea what to give him.

The following day, Little Miss Birthday decided that the simplest thing to do was to visit Mr Wrong, and hope that would give her a few ideas.

Mr Wrong lives in a house that … well, just looks wrong!

When Little Miss Birthday rang the doorbell, it did not go 'ding dong', it did not even buzz.

Do you know what noise it made?

It went: 'OINK, OINK!'

"Come in, come in," said Mr Wrong, as he answered the door and promptly stepped outside.

Mr Wrong and Little Miss Birthday made themselves comfortable in the garden.

They had a long conversation, none of which made any sense to Little Miss Birthday, but she did have a very nice time.

Though unfortunately, their chat left Little Miss Birthday no nearer to solving the problem of what to give Mr Wrong as a birthday present.

The next day, Little Miss Birthday went for a walk.

"What would Mr Wrong want more than anything else?" she asked herself, watching the autumn leaves blowing past.

"Morning, Mr Muddle," she said to Mr Muddle, who was on his way to the shops. Or was he on his way back? He could never be sure.

"Afternoon," replied Mr Muddle. "Lovely summer's day we're enjoying."

"But it's not summer ..." said Little Miss Birthday, and then she had an idea.

"Of course! Thank you Mr Muddle," she cried, and rushed off to organise Mr Wrong's birthday present.

A few days later, it was Mr Wrong's birthday.
Little Miss Birthday went round to Mr Wrong's house
with his present.

Mr Wrong had heard the doorbell, 'OINK! OINK!'
but he kept opening the wrong door.

He had opened the pantry door, the cupboard door
and the fridge door, before he finally opened the
front door.

"Goodbye! Goodbye!" greeted Mr Wrong.

He looked at Little Miss Birthday.

"You've brought me a present," he said.
"It must be …"

Before Mr Wrong could utter another word, Little Miss
Birthday cried, "Happy Christmas!" and gave him
a present wrapped in Christmas paper.

Mr Wrong stood holding the present in astonishment.

"I was just about to say it must be Christmas!
And … I was right!" he exclaimed.

Mr Wrong was over the moon. Little Miss Birthday
had given him the one thing he wanted more than
anything else.

Mr Wrong wanted to be right!

Mr Wrong tore the wrapping paper off Little Miss Birthday's present.

She had given him a sledge.

"It's fantastic!" cried Mr Wrong.
"I've always wanted a …"

"… bike!"

Little Miss Birthday just smiled.